MEMORIES NEVER FADE

LITTLE MOMENTS, BIG MEMORIES

DR. SAHITHI MANNEPALLI

XpressPublishing
An imprint of Notion Press

XpressPublishing
An imprint of Notion Press

Old No. 38, New No. 6
McNichols Road, Chetpet
Chennai - 600 031

First Published by Notion Press 2019

ISBN 978-1-64805-389-4

THIS BOOK IS DEDICATED TO

MY FATHER (Mr. HANUMANTHARAO GARU)

MY MOTHER(Mrs. SUMANA GARU)

MY BETTER HALF(Dr.SHANMUKH RAM)

Contents

Foreword *vii*

Preface *ix*

Acknowledgements *xi*

Prologue *xiii*

1. It Started Like That... 1
2. Life Is Beautiful... 6
3. That Night In The Pub... 13
4. Back In The Spooky Place... 17
5. Perpetual Perception 21
6. Down The Memory Lane... 25
7. Trepidation... 29
8. In Search Of Other People... 32
9. Five Of Us Together Again... 37
10. Reading Between The Lines... 41
11. Escape Plan... 45
12. Lesson Learned... 49

Foreword

Dedicated to all the friends out there who created memories for lifetime...

millions of memories,
thousands of words,
hundreds of smiles,
tens of fights,
and love for life.

Preface

GOOD TIMES AND CRAZY FRIENDS MAKE GREAT MEMORIES...

EVERYBODY COMES WITH A BAGGAGE, A BAGGAGE WITH TONS OF MEMORIES. THIS BOOK RELATES TO EACH AND EVERY EMOTION IN FRIENDSHIP. MEMORIES NEVER FADE...

Acknowledgements

I am really grateful for the ones who supported me and believed me at every point of time and who stayed with me through thick and thin.

I am thankful to Mr.P. Subrahmanyam garu, Mrs.Naga Jyothi garu for supporting me. special thanks to Mr.Saketh for believing in me.

I am thankful to my entire MANNEPALLI family for encouraging me.

Prologue

THIS BOOK "MEMORIES NEVER FADE" IS ALL ABOUT FRIENDS AND MEMORIES...

LET IT BE GOOD OR BAD, MEMORIES NEVER FADE.

CHEERS TO FRIENDS AND FRIENDSHIPS, BECAUSE OF YOU PEOPLE THERE IS LIVELINESS IN LIFE.

IF YOU HAVE SOME BEAUTIFUL FRIENDS IN YOUR LIFE ,YOU ARE DEFINETELY GOING TO RELATE TO THIS BOOK.

SOME PEOPLE ARRIVE AND MAKE SUCH A BEAUTIFUL IMPACT ON YOUR LIFE, YOU CAN BARELY REMEMBER WHAT LIFE WAS LIKE WITHOUT THEM. AND, YOU CALL THEM FRIENDS. "MEMORIES NEVER FADE" IS THAT KIND OF A BOOK THAT REFRESHES ALL YOUR MEMORIES YOU HAD WITH YOUR FRIENDS.

ONE

IT STARTED LIKE THAT...

"Anne, do you think something fishy is happening here?!!" whispered Alia and turned to see when she didn't receive any answer. She was horrified because she couldn't find her friends who came along with her.

"Anne, Jackkk...can anyone hear me!!!! Stop playing with me now and please come back,

I am really scared...Guysssssss!!!!"Alia started shouting. After going through all the rusty doors and dusty walls in the spooky darkness, that night. She neither found someone nor got a reply back. Sitting in complete darkness all the memories just flashed in her mind.

******

A Few months back, Me, Anne, Jack, Bella and, Fred was chilling out in " The madhouse cafe."

"Hey, have a look at this article." screamed Jack in excitement." why did you shout like that Jack? What is the matter ?!!!" exclaimed Anne..."I think this is the place we are waiting for

Ready to explore?! "winked Jack with a naughty smile and flipped the paper to us and left to get our favorite mocktails.

Danial"5 Bluecoracoes and 5 brownies, please !!! yes sir, on the way .

We are coming to this cafe from our graduation days. Four long years with these idiots is an adventure for me.time flies fast isn't, it?!!! It was my first day when I was waiting outside the lab feeling nervous to go inside. That was the time when I first met Anne. She is more like a boy rather than a girl with short hair and a walk full of attitude."Hey, this is Anne Richards. Are you new to this college??"

"oh hi! I am Alisha Nandan. And friends call me Alia. My father got transferred to this place a few days back so, I got my admission from this midterm".

"Ok Alia, so You are an Indian! great!! you are going to have great fun out here. Don't worry. come, let's go inside, I will introduce you to my friends."

"Hey guys !meet my friend Alia and Alia this is my gang Jack, Bella And Fred"

"silenceeeee!!!!!!!! A rough voice came from the background which sounded harsh. It is none other than our Bulldog. Sorry, I mean to say it is our professor Dr.Davidson whom we call Bulldog because of his arrogance.

Our lab session got completed and we all left our labs. we still had thirty minutes for the next session to be started. so, we all went to visit a cafe about 3 km from our campus gate. It is "The Mad House Cafe". It is a cool place to hang out with friends. our memories are allied with this cafe. our silly fights, gossips, presentations, breakups what not almost everything that can happen in four years of friendship. While I was still in my thoughts,

Jack arrived with our drinks and brownies." oh come on Jack!! do you think we have to explore this place?!! this place seems to be dangerous" said Bella."If not now, Never. This is going to be our last year in this college.so, let's do something big, something for a lifetime" said Fred.

"Yup, Fred is right!!!" echoed a voice from my back. It is Anne who went to check out the mirror for the hundredth time that day."Guys, don't you think Anne is becoming too girlish these days" winked Jack. And everybody

laughed all of a sudden." oh !very funny...now, shut up Jack or else I will kick you out.so, when are we getting started guys"asked Anne. "This Sunday" said Fred and walked away to settle the bill."Check please!" said Fred .then, came our very friendly waiter Danial. We call him Danny. This time the very silent Danny came up with a suggestion. We hardly heard him speaking all these years. Can you guess what he spoke to Fred?! He warned us about the place we planned to visit. Well! there were no proper reasons why we are not supposed to visit that place. but, I was somehow scared about this trip. I just felt some kind of uneasiness which I never felt all these days being a part of all the adventures till now. After deciding to leave next Sunday, every one of us left to pack our bags for our biggest adventure. even though everybody is excited, some unpleasant feeling is there in everyone's mind.

****

TWO

LIFE IS BEAUTIFUL...

That night I reached my home and started packing my bags. Deciding not to carry too much stuff, I landed up packing a pair of jeans and a few tees with me and of course! yes, how can I forget to carry my favorite sneakers Lastly, a handbag with a pack of tissues, my aviators and some random stuff I usually carry with me. When I opened my drawer to find my socks I came across a book. Yes, a scrapbook. which I got habituated to fill with my memories after each trip.

As I opened the first page of the book,

"That was my first semester holidays...never thought that we five are going to become so close. Like, friends for a lifetime.

While I was packing my bag to visit my aunt's place, my phone started ringing......

"Alia, it is me Anne, we are planning to go to the hilltop tonight. Want to join???!!" "well! maybe next time Anne. I am leaving to visit my aunt's place tonight. you guys carry on." "Ok then, see you" Anne hung up. Of course, I wanted to go out with them. I already started missing those idiots. Finally, I came out of all those thoughts and kept packing my things. After about an hour or so, our doorbell rang..... When I went opened the door."Jack!!!!! What are you doing here at this time????" I asked him surprisingly. "we came to kidnap you!!!!" a husky voice came from the other side. it was Bella. "what....!!!!!!!!!" By the time I could recover from the shock....my idiots launched me in the car along with my bag. Anne handed over my phone" Call your mom and inform that you are going on a road trip with your friends". I just smiled and called my Mom and Aunt. As I hung up and lifted my head, everyone is already staring at me with a smile on their lips. "now, what!!!" I asked.

"How can you plan something alone, My dear drama queen?! And, how can you even think that we are going to plan something leaving you behind?!" sighed Anne.

It took some time to settle down. I understood that I am fortunate enough to get such crazy friends in my life. It took about 6 hours for us to reach the hilltop. By the time we reached it was already dawn. We stopped at one place. I got out of the car to free myself from the cramps after a tiresome journey. It was foggy out there. The first thing I felt after getting down was a pleasant, happy and peaceful soul of mine relaxing looking at the very scenic nature that occupied my mind and heart in very little time. It was refreshing after all the stressful examinations, many sleepless nights and all the tensions. Felt as if I am the happiest person in this entire world. As I turned around I saw a lonely road with a huge tree at the end of the road. As it is spring season, the road is full of beautiful and colorful flowers as if, they are welcoming us to a more beautiful place. It just felt like heaven fell on to the earth in that particular place. All the others came to me feeling the same. At the same time, we were really tired and hungry ."It is already late!!!! Did you get anything to eat??" screamed Bella. "oh come on, Bella!! Let us search for a safe place to arrange our tents first .then, we can think about food" shouted back Jack and started searching for a place to fix our tents. As we walked along the lanes down that beautiful starry sky and a cool breeze that is frequently touching us to make us feel good.

We finally found a place where we can hardly see anything around in that darkness yet, it seems to be safe because there were few shops nearby. We fixed our tents and had some sandwiches and Ramen we bought with us. And, went into our tents to take rest. As soon as we laid down we fell asleep. "wakeup Aliaaaaa!!!" shouted Anne in excitement." Now, what is it! Why are you shouting, that too @ 5 AM??" I shouted back. "Wakeup Alia, we didn't come here to take a nap. Now, wakeup and get ready," replied Anne . when I came out of the tent with my half-opened eyes....

"Are you kidding me!!!! Now, don't tell me that we are going for a bungee jump." I shouted feeling horrified hoping that the answer would be a "No". " of course, we are, dear!" screamed Anne excitedly. "what????!!!!!! no ways...do not even expect me to come there". I replied with my fingers crossed because I can't trust these idiots, they are capable of throwing me down just like the way they pushed me into the car the day before.

"You don't have any other choice babes...." Said Fred. after about 30 minutes, I am at the edge of the mountain well equipped to take a long jump in a few seconds. "Do u guys have any second thoughts??? I am nervous ." I shouted at my friends who are a few meters away from

me." " No second thoughts dear!!! Replied my four idiots all at a time . It was spine chilling looking down from such higher altitudes and now, time to jump. I took a long breath and jumped. "Aaaaarrrrrrggghhhhhhhhhhhhhh" that was the last word that came from my mouth after jumping. After a few minutes, I am in the same place from where I jumped. "yes!!!!! I did it!! I did it!!!" never felt this much amazed. I just felt like my soul came out and started dancing like "Hurray, I did it !!!!!!!".Everyone took their chances and we were really happy about what we did. Later, that morning we took a long walk in that foggy way. Once we reached our destination we had our breakfast with the leftover plums, garlic bread and tomatoes we brought the day before." Now, what next?!!" exclaimed Anne. "How about camping tonight???!!" asked Fred. Everyone agreed with the idea.

That evening, another troop joined us. The first similarity I noticed about the other troop was the same joy and friendship among us. Yes, they were just like us. As usual, our boys started flirting with the girls in the other group. There was a campfire with songs which are perfect for camping. We danced, screamed as if we are mad, played till we got tired, ate till our stomachs are full, laughed till our stomachs started to hurt. That time, I felt "Life is beautiful, our choices decide our happiness. I am proud of myself that I have chosen them and fortunate enough that they have chosen me. We are lucky enough that we are together." Yes, friends, definitely define who you are, what you can be and they are the ones who will help you to become a better person. The next day morning, we packed our bags and removed our tents and started our journey back to the place where we belong. It was very hard for me to leave them."So, what are the plans for tonight?" I asked while getting down in front of my gate."How about a party tonight!" asked Jack. I just gave a wink and left. Within no time I got a message showing the time and place where we are going to party tonight.

THREE

THAT NIGHT IN THE PUB...

We reached our homes by the afternoon that day. as it was a tiring day I took a small nap. Later in the evening....my phone rang, it was Anne in a very excited voice "hey babes, what are you going to wear for the party tonight?!.

Me: well! I didn't think about it yet.

Anne: you dint think of it till now? come on dear, we have to leave in an hour.

Me: Yup! I know,

Anne: Ok, then decide quickly and get ready see you then, I will hang up for now, bye.

Me: bye Anne. See you in the evening

I hanged up and opened my wardrobe and started exploring my dresses. after ten minutes, I found a dress I bought in a sale a few months back. it is a pink frock with white lace and a beautiful neckpiece. I took my shower and changed into that pink frock, curled my hair and wore my 6 -inch wedges that are gifted by my mom on my birthday. all set to go to the party. "Are you ready to leave?" shouted Anne from our drawing-room. for the last time I looked at the mirror. "oh wait! I forgot to wear my lipstick .i took my peach-colored lipstick from the draw and applied it over my lips ". now, done. let us go". Anne was in her navy blue short skirt beautiful as always with long, straight hair. Later, at the party, all five of us are together again to have a blast tonight in the pub. Fred and Jack headed to the bar counter to get the drinks . we girls, started gossiping and chitchatting as always. The boys came back with a tray having 10 vodka shots. We had enough drinks and headed on to the dance floor. Fred and Jack started flirting with the girls around. At the same time when we were dancing, a boy entered the pub." Sorry sir, no entry for the stags." Guards stopped him at the door. "Do you know who I am?" that boy shouted back. The manager of the pub came running "sorry sir, these guards are new here. please come in." he screamed. "you are screwed!!!" shouted that guy in anger. "who do you think he is? He is the one and only son of our chairman. The prince of his whole empire. Now, leave this place before he kicks you out." Said the manager. even though that guy is rude, I liked his attitude. he is six feet tall with a perfect body, curly hair and a million-dollar smile which every girl would die for. he went to the bar counter and the bearer came up with a large peg of cocktail . he sat in a corner sipping that cocktail and watching people dance. I just felt that he is a loner with no friends. We left the pub @10;30. I came home thinking about the guy I saw in that pub.

Mom: hey Alia, did you hear this news?! Your sister is getting

married next week.

Me: wow! That is a great news mom. who is that guy? Do we know him?

Mom: well, he is Naina's schoolmate. they are dating each other from 5 years

Me: oh ..that is cool. So, when is the wedding

Mom: In a week.

Me: ok mom, can I invite my friends to the wedding?

Mom: yes, of course, you can dear said my mom and left to cook for my dad.

turning the pages down in the scrapbook I realized that it is 2 AM and should go to sleep because I had a lot of work to do to submit my assignment.

FOUR

BACK IN THE SPOOKY PLACE...

Tears started rolling down my cheeks thinking about all the happy days we lived. I heard a scream from nowhere saying " Help!", recognizing it as Bella's voice I started running towards the sound wave through the dusty parallel doors

Suddenly something fell on my back making a thud sound. My breathing started to feel heavy as I was scared to turn back and see what it is. Slowly, I turned back to see a dead bird. Breathing heavily I started running towards the other side and ran into something probably a person in that utter darkness.

Aarghhh!! I heard a sound in a high pitched voice. "Bella, it is me, Alia, stop shouting".

Bella: "save me, save me" she started crying.

Alia: " look at me, don't be scared"

Bella: "thank god Alia, I found you." She was horrified.

Her face had bruises on the head and upper lip, blood is oozing from nose. There was dirt all over her clothes and face, she was wearing a single shoe and her clothes are partially torn.

Alia: "what is all this Bella, what happened to you?

Bella: "I fell in to a pit not seeing it in the darkness. stayed there shouting for help "

Alia: " A pit! how come there is a pit in the house?"

Bella: " I don't know, I feel like something fishy is happening here, by the way where are others?"

Alia: " I have been searching for all of you for a very long time. but couldn't find any"

Bella: " we made a mistake, a dreadful mistake" she was still crying.

We sat in a corner tired of all the mess. I searched for a handkerchief to stop her bleeding and found a piece of paper. Yes, it is that paper which made us put ourselves into trouble today

"People go missing" it read,

In the premises of the city, 8 people go missing near the Vincent Churchill road. The investigation is going on, 4 people's clothes found near the abandoned bungalow at the end of the road. Clues team searching for more clues and further investigation is going on. CCTV footage shows 8 people entering the bungalow and not coming back.

FIVE

PERPETUAL PERCEPTION

While I was still reading through the newspaper, suddenly a thought flashed in my mind.

We attended a lecture a few days back by our professor Dr. Rachel, who is my inspiration. She is the topper of the university and at a very young age, she became head of the department. In her lecture, she told us about perceptions and it's effects on people's lives. everybody's success or failure depends upon their perception of life. Now in this situation, I can relate to her lecture.

According to her, about her life experiences, she used to be an over- enthusiastic kid when she was young. Where she used to feel very competitive and ended up into depression when she could not achieve even the smaller goals. One day, her teacher called her and explained to her about contentment.

Contentment is a state of happiness and satisfaction .simply, it means being happy with what you have.

similarly, one of the most successful doctors who is her colleague felt that life is all about growth and achievements. You should thrive for learning and experimenting. Yes, he is also true because he is an achiever having 18 patent rights for doing great in his career and experimenting on something nobody ever dared to experiment on.

We cannot say one is right and the other is not.it is all about one's perception and proper implementation.

Why am I relating it to my scenario right now? What is perception?

Perception is how something is regarded, understood or interpreted.perpetual perception is nothing but the changing perceptions.

Now, in our case, we should have been contented about our enjoyment. We went over the board and ended up ourselves into the menacing situations. I may not be right but this is what I feel right now.

Think out of the box but be aware where you are putting yourselves in to. Use your perception to help you grow and think out of the box in choosing your career and developing yourself not into something that lands you into treacherous situations.

Suddenly, we both heard some footsteps coming towards us. We both started panicking. It was a person. Even though it is a human being, we are not sure we can get help from them.

A light flashed on our faces. "Alia! Bella!" it was a familiar voice but not the one that is close to us." It is me, jones!"

Alia: Jones! How come you are here? How do you know that we are here?

Jones: jack called me and invited to join you people but, you guys left by the time I arrived.

Alia: Good to see you jones, we ran out of batteries for our torch. Do you have an extra torchlight with you?

Jones: I don't have an extra torchlight, but I can accompany you.

Alia: thankyou.

SIX

DOWN THE MEMORY LANE...

Do you remember the guy we spoke about who is the owner of a pub?

There is something suspicious about this guy from the day we first met him. We met this guy again at my sister's wedding that took place in Carolina. It was a perfect Christian wedding with Indian tadka. It is a proper beach wedding. Five of us along with my mom and dad reached the place. There Something is appealing about tying the knot in an exotic location and setting. What bride to be wouldn't want to stroll down the sandy aisle barefoot to her future husband? And just think

of those amazing pictures!

The venue is decorated beautifully with orchids, lilies, and freesias. There was this beautiful standing board depicting the beauty of the scene that is taking place which reads, " shoes here, vows there and love everywhere!!"

Then arrived my beautiful sister wearing a pretty white frock and long veil carried by her bride's maids. She looked like a perfect bride for me with happiness all over her face and love in her eyes. And, on the other side, it was the groom in a black colored three-piece suit with a masculine body and perfectly sculptured face.

As they exchanged their vows, that magical moment happened right there which can be seen in their eyes showing their love towards each other, which was pure and divine.

We moved on to a place where there was an authentic meal, my friends were busy tasting the spritzy wines and drooling salads. It was a huge buffet with all the mouth-watering dishes on the table. that was the time when my sister introduced us to Mr. Henry (bridegroom). A guy accompanying was Henry who is none other than Mr.charmer from the pub.

Henry: Alia, meet my cousin jones.

Alia: hi, I think I have seen you somewhere!

Henry: he is the most desirable man in the city, he owns a group of pubs in the city.

Alia: yeah! Maybe I saw him in one of them.

Jones: Nice to meet you, Alia.

I introduced Jones to my friends on that day and we kind of liked that guy at that moment. he joined us for parties sometimes. I always had a crush on this guy for which my friends made fun of me and I liked it more. There was this tattoo on his wrist on the left hand that symbolizes " Gypsy" that dint suit his character.

We had long talks, small walks, sweet smiles, and adorable words together that took me to the edge of heaven sometimes. Yes, I loved each

moment I spent with him but the bonding was not the same as that of my friends. There was some line that always existed between us that dint allows me to go further close

SEVEN

TREPIDATION...

Suddenly some weird sounds were coming through the windows, the sky is cloudy and dark without stars or moon. We have been stuck here for 20 hours for now. Spine chilling breeze made us shiver terribly that night. We neither had blankets to cover ourselves nor we know where we left our bags. It felt as if we are going to die out of chills. Its been more than a day since we had our last meal.

Three of us started walking in the endless path not knowing where to go and where to end. Walking through the way my leg got stuck in something not letting me move. As we flashed the light we saw it was a trap that caught my leg which made me cry hell out of my self.

Bella and jones tried taking my leg out of the trap and it started bleeding profusely. After trying so hard to remove it, finally, I am out of the trap with indentations and bleeding all over the leg. I started limping on one leg and searching for others waiting for the dusk to leave now.

Weird sounds started becoming intense and our ears could not bear them anymore as it is beyond the normal decibels. Somebody pushed jones from the back, as he reached the floor by the sudden jerk. We turned back to see if there is somebody finding there is no one.

We started trembling out of fear seeing all the unnatural things happening to us. As we progressed towards the other room and stepped inside we found ourselves locked from behind. We tried opening the door and failing to open it every time.

A strong pungent smell started fogging the room. We couldn't breathe as the smell was so strong and resembles that of a dead animal. When we tried to look at what it is into each and every corner of the room, we found a dump of clothes soaked in blood in one corner. They seemed like the clothes of the missing people. Collecting all the courage we have we started digging through the clothes to find a half decomposed dead body.

Astonished by the sight of the dead body, we started knocking the closed door to get out of the room. All of a sudden the door hung open on its own and we started running directionless.

After running for so long, we found ourselves in the center of the house. As we started moving forward, we saw a skeleton hanging from the ceiling. That didn't scare me anymore because being a science student we know the difference between an artificial and a natural one. Bella was still scared because her mind is preoccupied with the fear of supernatural forces.

EIGHT

IN SEARCH OF OTHER PEOPLE...

I and Bella started searching for others including jones. Jones left his torchlight with us which made our search easy. My leg started paining like hell because of the trap. The bleeding didn't stop yet and my leg started turning black.

We sat near the stairs to cover my let to stop bleeding. I sat on the stairs and Bella started wrapping the scarf around my leg. Suddenly, we heard knocking sounds coming from somewhere. Alia: " Wait a minute, do you hear anything? "

Bella: *" Yeah, seems like somebody is knocking the door. "*

Alia: *" Bella it can be one of our friends. " we started shouting " Fred! Jack! Anne! Jones! "*

The knocking got intensified.

Alia: *" I think it is this way, come on let us go, but be careful. "*

Bella: *" the sound is coming from the storage underneath the stairs. "*

Alia: *" come on let us go and check. "*

As we came to see near the storage the door was locked from outside. As we started shouting to find out whether it is one of our friends and found out that it was Fred and Anne.

Alia: " guys hold on, we are finding ways to get you out of it. Bella, can you please get something hard to open the lock? "

Bella: " Wait, there is a stone over there, let me get it. "

As we started hitting on the lock to break it open, we found out that it was really strong and hard to open it. But we are not the ones who are going to let things go easily. And that too it was our friends who are on the other side. So we tried hard for some time. On our tenth or eleventh attempt, we broke the lock open and relieved our Fred and Anne from that shady room.

Alia: " How come you guys are here and who locked you here? "

Fred: " We don't know who it is. We went unconscious as somebody hit us from the back and ended up locked in this room. "

Alia: " what! Who did that to you? "

Anne: " something fishy is happening here."

Bella: " I already told you guys that we should not go against supernatural powers. "

Anne: " Stop being stupid Bella. It is not something supernatural. It is our very own human beings doing illegal deeds in the name of supernatural forces. "

Alia: " How can you say that? "

Anne started telling us the story about how they got locked in the room and what they have seen.

Anne: " When I and Fred separated from you guys after entering the house we went directionless not knowing whom to ask and where to search. In the process, we went into the back yard. And to our surprise, we saw four people digging a huge pit that can cover even a hefty man. When we tried looking who they are, they started chasing us. We started running towards the house and Fred fell as he stepped on to a log of wood. Getting on to his feet back we started running into the house through the back door. I accidentally fell on to

the wall. Later we saw a staircase leading to the underground."

"We slowly started going downstairs to find the passage, which leads to four other rooms. As we tried peeking into one of the rooms to see men packing few boxes.

" Suddenly somebody blew on to both of our heads and we don't know what happened the next minute. "

Alia: " do you know where is that room? "

Anne: " yes. "

NINE

FIVE OF US TOGETHER AGAIN...

We four started searching for Jack, now it is almost 2'0 clock in the night. With our empty stomach, tired eyes and dirty clothes, we started going to all the corners of the house in search of the jack.

Anne: " Hey, somebody is hiding behind the box."

Alia: " Wait, don't do there, they might harm you. "

Fred: "Let me search for something to defend if somebody attacks".

We found around and kept it for our safety. As we started walking towards the box, slowly taking step by step in the pin-drop silence. Suddenly a person attacked us, with a stick once we moved the box. As Fred was ready to attack him back, Bella shouted saying " Wait Guys it is Jack. "

She recognized as she flashed the light on to his face.

Jack:" Guys! Thank god! you guys are here. "

Alia: " Jack, are you ok ??"

Jack:" Yes, I am fine. Guys, I have a piece of big news. "
Fred: "Good to have all of us safe." He said as he hugged jack tightly.

Alia:" tell me what is the thing ?"

Jack: " Not here, let us go to a safe place first".

We went into a corner room and locked ourselves from inside. Sitting on the floor forming a circle, we started telling what had happened to each of us.

Jack: " I found a cam recorder in the pit downstairs. People started chasing me to destroy the recorder. I somehow managed to save myself and the recorder. I think it can help us to find the clues to solve this case. "

Fred: " Now let us watch what is there inside."

Anne: " Make sure there is no voice because it can get us into trouble. "

As we started watching the video

Alia: " It seems like one of the missing persons recorded it. "

A person started at the beginning of the video, who seems to be a reporter who went missing. There was utter silence as the video progress.

It shows a few people packing the boxes with drugs.

Alia: " Wait a minute! "

Bella: " what is it now? "

Alia: " can u look at the tattoo on that man's hand? "

Fred: " So? "

Alia: " I have seen it Somewhere. "

TEN

READING BETWEEN THE LINES...

After completely watching the video, we started discussing it.

Jack: " So now there is no ghost or supernatural power here. "

Anne: " they are scaring away people so that there will be no obstacle for their business. '

Alia: " Yeah! If we start reading between the lines, we can find the clues. "

Fred: " You are right. "

Bella: " Guys stop it now. Please see the way for us to escape. Why do you want to get into this? "

Alia: "No Bella, we came till here to crack the case and we are almost there. It is meaningless if we leave it here and go. "

Bella: " But don't you understand these people can harm us. "

Alia: " We promise you that we will keep you safe through all this. "

1.

They hanged the bird and arranged it near the door in such a way that when somebody opens the door, the bird falls on them which scares them away.

2.

A pit in the middle of the house depicts two things either to trap a person or to hide something.

3.

A trap is used to catch or lock a person there.

4.

All those dirty clothes are used to cover a dead body.

5.

An artificial skeleton to scare people.

There is indeed a mastermind behind all of these.

And the tattoo ?!

Alia: " wait I have seen the same tattoo on Jone's hand, which is the same as that of the one that is seen in the video. It is a gypsy tattoo. "

Bella: " By the way, where is Jones? He was with us two hours back "

Jack: " Jones! Why is Jones here? "

Alia: " What? You invited jones to come with us, Didn't you? "

Jack: " why would I even do that? "

Alia: " Wait, now I get it, so you didn't invite jones to the adventure, but he is here. He neither hurt nor his clothes was dirty. He acted as if he also one of the victims. The tattoo we saw in the video was the same as that of jones. It must be jones who is behind all of this. "

Fred: " What! He doesn't seem like that. "

Anne: " If you read between the lines, yes she is right."

ELEVEN

ESCAPE PLAN...

Jack: " I think we should approach the police. "

Anne: " Two of us will go to the police and the other three will see that none of them escapes from here. "

Fred: " Yes, lets us do that. "

Anne: " We can go from the backdoor, climb the wall and reach the other side. I know the way, let's go. "

Jack: " Fred and Bella you guys go to the police and explain to them what has happened. We three will stay here and see that those idiots won't escape. "

Fred: " Will do! "

It was around 4'0 clock in the morning as we slowly started walking towards the back door, and started searching for a stool or ladder for them to cross the wall. We found a huge drum by which we successfully manage to cross the wall.

Jack: " Now let us find the room where they are packing the drugs. "

We started walking back into the house to find the stairs that led to the passage. As we went to the place where Anne first saw the staircase.

Anne: " What! We saw the staircase right here last time. "

Jack: " If it is here it has to be here now also, Right! "

Anne: " That is what I am not understanding. "

As I leaned towards the wall some irregularity was touching my back. That slowly started moving.

Alia: " Guys look! "

Suddenly the door of the staircase started opening. We went down slowly removing the shoes not to make noise and entered the passage. As we progressed towards the room we saw the people still working. We locked the door from outside and waited for the police to arrive. Fred and Bella reached the place along with the police to expose the criminals.

As the police removed the masks, it was Jones along with few other people.

Alia: " I knew it! "

Jones: "U are going to pay for it. "

Police: "Only if you are out of the jail alive."

We reached the police station. They investigated us and warned us not to do such things again. They rescued the other seven people and carried forward with the investigation about the dead body.

We are finally out of this. This incident was buried among the five of us. We neither spoke about it nor try to do such things again.

TWELVE

LESSON LEARNED...

Even though we came out of the house alive and experienced the thrill we learned a lesson, a lesson for the life-time, that we should not put our selves into risk and go beyond board to enjoy.

Now, we are all grown up and matured leading our busy lives happy and contented, we can never forget the agony and pain we went through in those days.

Yes, we had memories, let it be good or bad.

MEMORIES NEVER FADE.

www.ingramcontent.com/pod-product-compliance
Lightning Source LLC
LaVergne TN
LVHW090136160826
845673LV00017B/2485

* 9 7 8 1 6 4 8 0 5 3 8 9 4 *